The Cottage at Deer Crossing

Sharon E. Jellel

AuthorHouse™
1663 Liberty Drive
Bloomington, IN 47403
www.authorhouse.com
Phone: 833-262-8899

This book is printed on acid-free paper.

ISBN: 979-8-8230-3525-5 (sc)
ISBN: 979-8-8230-3527-9 (hc)
ISBN: 979-8-8230-3526-2 (e)

Library of Congress Control Number: 2024921657

Print information available on the last page.

Published by AuthorHouse 12/20/2024

authorHOUSE®

Acknowledgements

This book is dedicated to my husband, Douglas, my 4 children: Christopher, Ashley, Eric, Josh (Chaserjo)

It is also dedicated to my 6 granddaughters, Kylie, Ellie, Rylee, Charlotte, Elaina and Evelyn, who are all mentioned in my book.

I t was a stormy night. The wind was blowing hard outside the little village of Chevel in Kyelry County. It had been a beautiful day soaking up all the sunshine as the townspeople shopped at the businesses that were lined up on both sides of Tuit Lane.

Some were at the general store, some were at the bakery, some were at the church or library, some were at the train station or barber shop and others were at the farmer's market. Mrs. Mogami was the last shopper to leave. She returned her books to the library and checked out several more, then hurried to the train station to catch the next train to her cottage. When the train dropped her off at the station closest to her cottage, she waved goodbye to Everest the engineer and rushed to her cottage as the rain continued. Everest had been driving the train for as long as she could remember.

Mrs. Mogami lived in a little cottage in the woods where deer came to eat every evening. She would feed them corn and would always leave some for the squirrels and rabbits. She also fed the birds. She was glad to have the rain because her zinnias needed water. Every evening, she would make sure her zinnias had plenty of water to make sure they grew. The colors of the flowers were beautiful and she enjoyed looking at them every morning. The yellow ones were her favorite. Everyone complimented her on her flowers and suggested she enter them in the contest that the townspeople were doing in just 3 months. If only she could……

The mayor had asked all the townspeople to come up with projects that they thought would be the best for the little village of Chevel. Major Lugi decided that there would be a contest to see who could do the best for the people of Kyelry County. Not every project would be chosen, but Mayor Lugi had asked all the townspeople to come up with different projects. He would choose a panel of judges to see which projects would win.

Mrs. Mogami knew she would not be able to enter a project because she had not been able to get around very well lately. Ever since she had fallen and hurt her knees 2 years ago, she had not been able to do all the things that she used to do. She had been the manager of the local school cafeteria for many years. She missed seeing all the kids every day. She also missed all the cooking she did. The kids loved her taco salad, homemade croutons, angel food cake and sugar cookies. She also helped in the nurse's station if one of the kids got sick or injured. It had been a great job but she could no longer do it because of her knees.

As the storm continued, Mrs. Mogami hurried to get her chairs out of the rain and find her cat Smokey. He loved to go outside and visit all the neighbor's houses, but he did not like the rain. Smokey came running to the porch of the little cottage to get out of the rain. "There you are!" said Mrs. Mogami. "I was getting worried about you!" As she went back in the house, she closed the windows, fed Smokey and pondered on the idea of using her zinnias for the project for Kyelry County. All the Townspeople had been so kind to her since she had accidently fallen and hurt her knees. Some people would bring her groceries, others would take her to the doctor's office and others would bring her books from the library.

Smokey followed her into the small kitchen of her cottage while she made some hot tea. Smokey curled up on the floor as Mrs. Mogami sat and enjoyed her tea and watched the rain. After a few minutes, the rain stopped and there was a beautiful rainbow. Mrs. Mogami stepped outside to have a better look. The rainbow was beautiful, and a wonderful reminder of God's promises. She stood there for a long time still thinking about the town project and wondering if she should enter the contest. She could teach people to grow the zinnias from seeds, then as they began to grow, she could show the townspeople how to water them and care for them and make sure they did not water them too much. They could be sold to the local florists and the townspeople could enjoy them as much as she did. She would have to give this idea a lot of thought. She did not like people helping her or feeling sorry for her.

And so, the contest began as many of the townspeople prepared their projects to make improvements to the little village of Chevel. They had just 3 months to complete their project before Mayor Lugi reviewed them. One by one each person would present their projects for improving Kyelry County to Mayor Lugi.

One of the townspeople was very eager to start her project. After much thought, Kylie decided that the most important thing for the people of Kyelry County was to make sure everyone had enough food to eat.

She invited all the people who had volunteered to help her with the project to a meeting at the library at 3:00 on Saturday. She laid out all the information for them to think about and discussed her plan with them.

She told them that they would need lots of canned goods, lots of fresh fruits and vegetables and lots of baked goods. She met with the farmers and asked if they would donate some of their crops. She also asked the dairy farmers to donate milk and butter. They agreed to help with this very worthy cause.

She told all the volunteers to go to each business and ask for donations to feed the hungry. They were all to meet back at the town square on Tuit Lane in seven days to put the baskets together to pass them out to people who needed food.

All the volunteers worked around the clock, visiting businesses, calling merchants and sending e-mails to neighbors and friends to give donations of food for Kylie's project. The day arrived that they were to put the baskets together. It took many hours to finish filling all the baskets.

They were given all the food from the county fair at the end of each day, which helped a lot. There were fresh fruits, vegetables, fresh baked pies, cookies and cakes. There were homemade jams, jellies and preserves donated by Mrs. Stiltner's corner market.

They also had donations of juice, milk and lots of other items to distribute. When the day was done, they had more than enough boxes of food to pass out to the hungry people in Kyley County. They even had enough to start a food pantry and set up volunteers to work so that when people needed food they could go there and get as much as they wanted. As they were finishing up on the last day of the project, Kylie noticed Mrs. Mogami standing at one of the tables. Kylie asked her if she needed food. The woman said "No, thank you, Kylie. I was just looking at how much work you've done for your project." Kylie thanked her as she headed for the door.

Yes, it had been a good idea to focus on hunger and make that her Project. Kylie was very happy that she had decided to make this her project since it was the biggest need in Kyelry County. All she needed now was a permanent place to have the food pantry and she was sure to win the contest.

Ellie was the next person to present her project to help the people of Kyelry County. "For my project, I would like to have a free medical clinic set up for everyone who cannot afford to go to the doctor," said Ellie. "I think my project will be the most needed for the people of Kyelry county. While I agree with Kylie that feeding the hungry is very important, I think that a free medical clinic would be great."

"Anyone who goes to the clinic will be given free exams and no one will be given a bill. I intend to contact all the doctors in the area and the surrounding counties to see if they would be willing to donate their time to start up a free clinic and to also give out free medicine to those who need it."

And so, Ellie began her outreach to all the neighboring counties. She had great results. All the doctors and even some of the nurses agreed that they would donate a few hours every week to help start up the free clinic. Anyone who came in with a broken arm, sore throat, cough, sunburn or anything else, would be treated at no cost.

As the sick people gathered in the local gym that had been set up as a temporary clinic, Ellie knew that her project would be the best for the people of Kyelry County. She just needed a permanent place to have the free clinic. As she was heading down Tuit Lane, she noticed a woman sitting on the bench outside the place where the doctor had set up for free exams. Ellie asked the woman if she was waiting to see the doctor. The woman replied "No, I was just sitting here watching all the people attend the free clinic." Ellie told her she could sit on the bench as long as she wanted. She continued down Tuit Lane with excitement in her heart just thinking about the new Clinic and free medical care. Yes, Ellie was sure to win the contest once Mayor Lugi heard about it.

Rylee was the next to talk about her project. "Both of you had great ideas about the need in Kyelry County. It is important to feed the hungry as Kylie said, and it's equally important to have free medical care as Ellie said. But I believe that my project is equally important. I think that everyone in the village of Chevel should know how to read. Reading is such an important thing and will be most valuable to the people." Yes, this no doubt was the right choice and Rylee was sure to win the contest.

And so, Rylee set out to accomplish her goal of teaching everyone to read. She contacted the local teachers and the librarian and asked for their help. They all agreed to help because they knew that this was a very important need in Kyelry County. They lined up all the volunteers and they were to meet at the library at 1:00 on Saturday.

Each volunteer would sit at a table and if anyone came in that needed to learn how to read, they would tutor them. So many people showed up that they had to set up another table outside the library. Then another table had to be set up and before long there were tables lined up on both sides of the library parking lot. Rylee noticed a woman looking at all the books. Rylee asked the woman if she would like to borrow one of the books. The woman just replied, "No, thank you, I was just admiring all the people who wanted to learn how to read." Rylee told her to have a nice day and finished taking the last of the books back to the library as the woman went on her way.

Yes, it was a very successful tutoring session. When they were done with the class some of the pupils were doing speed reading. They loved reading so much that the library had to borrow more books from the neighboring libraries. This was surely the best thing that she could do for the townspeople of Kyelry County and all she had to do now was find a permanent place to have the reading classes each week. She was sure to win the contest.

The next person to present her project was Charlotte. "I think that all three of you have had terrific ideas on how to improve Kyelry County. Yes, feeding the hungry, making sick people well and teaching people to read are very important things and we can certainly use all of them, but I think we need a good Sports team in Chevel Village. I propose that we form an amazing sports team, so that we can introduce sportsmanship to everyone. Sports help to build confidence, responsibility and Leadership skills. It will help bring in more money when we sell tickets so it will help the village of Chevel to make improvements to the roads and we will not have to increase taxes," said Charlotte. Yes, this is by far the right decision for the people of Kyelry County

So, they decided to start a football team. This was going to be so much fun. They had a bake sale to raise money for the uniforms. They would need a left tackle, a running back, a wide receiver and a quarterback. They got the best football players from the high school to participate. They got Eric who was the left tackle, Christopher, who was the running back, Josh who was the wide receiver and Nathan who was the quarterback. Yes, they would be sure to raise a lot of money so they could keep the taxes down.

They gathered everyone on the team together and had their first practice. They practiced for a very long time and were tired when they finally finished. It was time for their first game. They had a tough opponent, but they were sure that they could win the game. They hired an incredibly famous coach who knew everything about football, He played in the championship game when their team won the State Championship title many years ago. He would choose the right people to play and the right people to sit on the benches. His name was Coach Jellel, but most people called him Papa Jellel. He came from far away just to help with this worthy cause. They won their first game and sold many tickets, so Charlotte would be sure to win the contest as soon as she found a permanent place to hold the practices. Charlotte looked out at the bleachers and saw a woman sitting there all alone. Charlotte walked over to her and asked if she needed anything. The woman said "No, I was just watching to see how well the team played" and hurried on her way. Charlotte did not know what the woman's name was but hoped she would continue to come to the games. She could not wait to see who the winner of the contest would be. She just knew that she would be the winner.

The next person to present her project was Elaina. "I believe that Kylie's project for feeding the hungry, Ellie's project for free medical care, Rylee's project for teaching people to read and Charlotte's project for introducing sports are all great ideas, but I think we have another great need in our community, and I plan to do use it for my project", said Elaina. "I want to start a shelter for animals who have been abandoned."

There are so many horses, rabbits, dogs, and cats who do not have good homes and need to have someone who cares about them.

Stray animals cause many problems in the community. Not only can they have poor health, but they can cause problems for others. If they are not getting their vaccinations, they can spread diseases to wildlife and humans. If they are scared, they can cause property damage and if they are abandoned on the road, they can cause car accidents.

There was much work to do getting an animal shelter started. She had to find a location for the shelter, she had to get volunteers to help take care of the animals, she needed to get a veterinarian to examine the abandoned animals and get them up to date on their vaccinations and they needed to find people who were willing to adopt the animals once they were healthy.

And so, Elaina began her project. She made a newsletter and sent it to all the townspeople, she sent letters to the local veterinarians and asked for free medical care for all the animals. She also asked for donations of pet food for the animals. They would also need pet toys and someone to walk the dogs and others to feed all the animals.

They received great news from one of the local veterinarians who said he would give free medical care to all the animals. She also received news that the local supermarket would donate all the pet food for 90 days! This was wonderful news. The only thing they needed was an office manager who would set up an office and would help all the people who wanted to adopt an animal fill out all the forms.

Elaina decided that they would need to charge a small fee for the animals who were adopted and use that money to buy more food and supplies for the animals.

At last, everything was set up and the animal shelter was open for business. The first animal that came to the shelter was a dog. Elaina decided to name her Chloe. Several people wanted to adopt her because she was losing her eyesight and hearing. The next animal was a bunny and they decided to name him Buckeye. Elaina was sure that he would be adopted soon because he was so friendly. He loved carrots and hay. Elaina saw a lady standing by the arena where the animals were playing. She went over to ask if she wanted to adopt one of the animals. She simply said, "No, thank you," and went on her way. Elaina told her that she could come back any time she wanted to and visit the animals.

Yes, Elaina's project has been a huge success. The animals were all healthy and could be adopted. Her project was sure to win the contest when Mayor Lugi heard about it.

The next person on the list to show her project was Evelyn. "I think you have all had great ideas. We do need someone to take care of the animals and we need to feed the hungry, have free medical care, teach people to read and have sports teams," said Evelyn, "but I have another idea that I believe will be of great use to the people of Kyelry County."

 I want to start a cooking school where everyone will learn to cook the right foods to nourish their bodies, and I have the perfect chefs to help me start this cooking school.

Evelyn had a lot of work to do to start a cooking school. She would need pots and pans, recipes, healthy ingredients and a taste testing area set up. She intended to get volunteers to help do the taste testing. Fresh fruits and vegetables were the perfect choice for healthy foods.

Evelyn wanted to get help from some personal chefs that she had heard of to teach the townspeople how to cook healthy foods. The first chef would be Chef Heidi, all the way from Texas. Evelyn contacted her and asked for her help. Chef Heidi said she would love to teach a cooking class. She could make her delicious healthy banana muffins. She was asked to put the recipe in a cookbook that had recipes from across the United States.

She would make sure that no ingredients were left out of these delicious muffins and they would be the right choice for a healthy food. She was honored to be cooking alongside the other famous chefs. They came from the North and South and all about and had received many awards for their cooking skills.

The next Chef would be Chef Abigail from Utah. She would be making her famous short ribs and pasta. She traveled the world but never tasted anything quite so good. They were cooked very slowly to make sure they were just right. She reached out to the local farm to order the freshest beef for these yummy ribs! Only the freshest would do for this fabulous recipe.

The next Chef would be Chef Jill all the way from Indiana. She would be making her healthy lasagna. She would choose the freshest ingredients for this pasta dish, and so she contacted the owner of the wheat field and asked for his freshest wheat to make her homemade pasta. It was going to be so tasty and she could not wait for the classes to begin. This recipe was chosen for the nationwide cookbook as well.

And last but certainly not least is Chef Ashley from Tennessee. She will be teaching us how to make her famous sugar cookies. She makes these cookies every holiday and there are never any leftovers. She would teach the class how to use the freshest organic ingredients.

After several days of cooking, baking and taste testing, the cooking class had their grand opening. They got lots of registration cards and they had a full class on the first night. Evelyn saw a lady standing outside the door and asked if she would like to join the cooking class, but the lady said no as she walked down the hallway. Evelyn hoped that she would come to the next class, since it went so well. Yes, Evelyn was sure to win the contest for the most needed project in Kyelry county.

And so, with only 2 days left before Major Lugi looked at the projects and chose the winner, the townspeople began preparing for the grand event. There would be food trucks on Tuit Lane with a marching band for entertainment. There would be popcorn, peanuts and cotton candy for people to buy. Everyone was anxious to see who the winner of the town's project would be. Kylie decided to get the other 5 people together and have lunch. It was such a beautiful day so they decided to eat outside at the little café on Tuit Lane.

They all wished each other good luck with the contest and hoped that whatever project was chosen, that it would help the people of Kyelry County. As they were finishing their lunch, they saw Mrs. Mogami get off the train and head for the library.

Kylie told the others that Mrs. Mogami had come to watch as they made up the food baskets to feed the hungry. Ellie mentioned that she had also come to the free clinic but didn't need medical care. Rylee said, "Oh, she came to the library when I was doing my reading class too". "Really," said Charlotte, "she came and sat on the bleachers when we had our football practice too." Elaina spoke up as well. "She came to see me at the animal shelter and was looking at all the animals." Evelyn said she had come to the cooking class as well.

"I wonder why she came to see all of our projects," said Charlotte. "Maybe she entered the contest as well", said Elaina. "We should ask her if she wants to join us for lunch", said Rylee.

"That's a great idea," said Kylie. "Oh wait, here she comes now." They all looked down Tuit Lane as Mrs. Mogami headed their way with a load of books in her arms. "Hi Mrs. Mogami, would you like to join us for lunch?" asked Kylie. "Oh hello Kylie…..No, I'm sorry I won't be able to," said Mrs. Mogami. "I need to get home to water my Zinnias. They can't go very long without water and I've spent a lot of time in the library so I really must be going but thank you for the invitation." "We noticed you at some of our projects," said Ellie. "Are you going to enter a project for Mayor Lugi to review?" "Oh no," said Mrs. Mogami, "I was just admiring all the work that you all have done on YOUR projects. You all did a great job. I wish I could enter, but since I had a fall last year, my knees are bad and I'm unable to do some of the things I used to do."

"I'm sorry to hear that," said Rylee. "Me too", said Charlotte and Elaina. "Hey, I have a great idea. Why don't we help you do your project?" said Evelyn. "How about it you guys, can we do it?" "Hey yeah, we could help," said all the girls.

"Oh, I couldn't ask you to do that. It's way too much trouble," said Mrs. Mogami.

"It wouldn't be any trouble at all," said Kylie. "All our projects are done so we have time to help you. There are still 2 more days before the deadline." "Yes," said Charlotte, "WE would be happy to help you! Do you have an idea for a project?"

"Well, yes," said Mrs. Mogami. "I do. I was thinking about starting classes on how to care for flowers and vegetable gardens. I have beautiful Zinnias that I care for every day, but I would feel bad having all of you help me. I don't want to bother anyone."

"It won't be a bother", said Ellie. "We would love to help you. "Of course we would, said Rylee, and I think your idea would be very good for the people of Kyelry County. We could start a community garden that not only has your beautiful zinnias but also fresh fruits and vegetables." "Yes," said Evelyn, "we need lots of fresh fruits and vegetables for my project of cooking healthy meals, and Kylie's project for feeding the hungry could benefit from it as well!"

"I don't know what to say", said Mrs. Mogami. "If you're sure it won't be any trouble, I would love for you to help me. There's lots of things to do. We would need to consider what we are going to plant, we would need to clear the ground, test the soil and other things. Would you all be able to come to my house this afternoon to help me plan out my project? I live in the little cottage at Deer Crossing."

"Yes," said Ellie, "we would love to come to your cottage to help you plan your project! What time would you like us to be there? If you would like, we can follow you home now." All the others agreed and Mrs. Mogami was thrilled.

When they arrived at Mrs. Mogami's cottage, Smokey was waiting to be fed and so were the deer and birds. Mrs. Mogami quickly set out to feed all the animals. She wanted as much time as possible to plan her project with her new friends.

While she fed the animals, the girls looked around. "What a beautiful cottage," said Kylie. "I love the fireplace. It looks so cozy." "It sure does," said Ellie, "just look at all the beautiful vases of zinnias she has." "Oh and look at all her pots and pans in the kitchen, and all the beautiful dishes," said Rylee. "I never even knew this cottage was here," said Charlotte, "The yard is so big and look at all the fields in the back!" "You're right," said Elaina, "there are so many fields and so many small buildings too!" "Are you thinking what I'm thinking?" said Evelyn. "Yes I think we all are," said all the other girls!

" I think this is the perfect location for ALL our projects." said Evelyn. "We could use one of the buildings for the food pantry for my project," said Kylie. "Yes, and we could use another building for the free clinic, that was my project," said Ellie. "This is great, and we could use one of the buildings to hold a reading class each week for my project," said Rylee. "That's a great idea"! said Charlotte, "and with all the open fields, we could use them for the football team to practice on". "Oh, and we could use one of the buildings for the animal shelter that I chose for my project," said Elaina. "These are wonderful ideas," said Evelyn, "and we could use one of the buildings to hold my weekly cooking classes!"

"Let's tell Mrs. Mogami about our idea and see what she thinks." Said Kylie. They all ran out to meet Mrs. Mogami and told her what their ideas were. "Of course you can use anything on my property for your projects. Let's make a list so we don't leave anything out."

They followed Mrs. Mogami into her kitchen and she gave them her famous sugar cookies with lemonade. "These cookies are delicious, Mrs. Mogami," said Kylie. "Oh, thank you," said Mrs. Mogami. "I made these cookies for years when I was the lunchroom manager at the high school."

"You were the lunchroom manager?" said Ellie. "Yes, I was" said Mrs. Mogami, "and I enjoyed it so much. The kids would come in and say Good Morning to me every day, especially the football players. They loved my sugar cookies. I sure do miss all the kids and all the cooking, but I have not been able to do it and a lot of the other things I used to do because of my knees. I also helped as the school nurse. I feel bad that I'm not able to do the things I enjoyed for so many years." Mrs. Mogami went to get paper and a pencil to make the list for the girls.

While she was gone, the girls all looked at each other and began smiling. They all had another great idea at the same time. Charlotte was the first to mention it to the others. They were so excited to tell Mrs. Mogami what they planned to do. So, one by one each person told Mrs. Mogami what their idea was.

"Mrs. Mogami, we have a great idea," said Rylee. "Since you were the high school cafeteria manager, you could oversee Evelyn's cooking classes. You've had lots of experience knowing just how much to cook and which ingredients are the freshest and healthiest."

"Yes, and since you do such a good job raising zinnias as well as vegetables in your garden, you could also help organize the food pantry for Kylie's project. The community garden would need someone to make sure the plants got watered on a regular basis and you have the most knowledge", said Charlotte.

"And since you also helped with the nurse's station at the school, you could give your advice for the free clinic that Ellie wants to start," said Elaina. "You could treat minor cuts, bruises and other injuries."

"That's right Mrs. Mogami," said Ellie, "and since you feed the deer and birds, you would be great to work at the animal shelter that Elaina wants to start. Your love for animals would be so good for the shelter."

"And we all know how much you enjoy reading," said Charlotte. "We see you at the library all the time. You could help with the reading classes that Rylee wants to start."

"Your knowledge of minor injuries would be helpful for the Football team that Charlotte wants to start and you know most of the team." said Kylie.

"So, what do you say, Mrs. Mogami, would you be willing to help with all these projects?" Said Elaina.

Mrs. Mogami was speechless as tears began to fill her eyes. "You have all made me feel so needed. Thank you for making me feel appreciated again. Your encouragement and support have given me confidence that I can do all these things. So yes, I would love to oversee and volunteer at each of your projects."

"Great!" said Evelyn. "Now let's figure out how to get your zinnias entered in the project before the deadline." And so the friends all worked until almost nighttime, digging, planting and watering the zinneas. By the time they were done, they were very tired but they had made the deadline. Mrs. Mogami's project was sure to win the contest and be the biggest help for Kyelry County.

And so, the day came when the village of Chevel would celebrate Mayor Lugi's decision for the best project to improve the town. There was a panel of judges all taking notes as each contestant presented their project. All around the village were sounds of laughter as the people gathered to watch the town parade. Some were visiting the petting zoo, riding the rides, or visiting the funnel cake stands. Yes it was a grand time for the people of Chevel.

"May I have your attention please," said Mayor Lugi. The crowd became very quiet as they listened to the mayor. "We have chosen the winner for the project that we feel would do the most good for the village of Chevel. We have chosen Mrs. Mogami's project for the zinnia and vegetable garden." There were loud cheers and applause from the crowd of people who had gathered to hear the announcement.

"Now hold on everyone", said Mayor Lugi. "There's more! As you remember at the start of the contest 90 days ago, I said that there could be more than one winner, so today, we have chosen several other winners. First, Kylie's project to start a food pantry for the hungry wins." Everyone shouted and applauded. The mayor kept talking. "Next, Ellie's project for having a free medical clinic has also won. More shouts and applause could be heard from the crowd as the mayor continued. "Next, Rylee's project for teaching people to read also won." The people were so excited that they could be heard all around the town. "Next," said Mayor Lugi, "is Charlotte's choice for having a football team to promote teamwork." "Yay," said all the people. Next, the mayor announced that Elaina's project to start an animal shelter had also won. The crowd was applauding louder than ever as Mayor Lugi announced the next winner. "And finally, is the healthy cooking class chosen by Evelyn. That project won as well."

The girls went to the mayor and whispered something to him. Mayor Lugi shook his head in agreement and made another announcement.

"May I have your attention please?" said Mayor Lugi. "I have just been informed that Mrs. Mogami will be overseeing all the projects thanks to her skills over the years. Mrs. Mogami, can you come up to the platform to receive your trophy?" She made her way to the platform and after she accepted the trophy, she thanked the mayor and the panel of judges. "I want to express my gratitude, humility and appreciation for the people of Chevel for your help over the past months, as I have been unable to do a lot of things. I am blessed to be surrounded by the most amazing people. You have all helped me out with your caring and compassion. I especially want to thank my six new friends who have taught me a lesson in commitment, determination, confidence and kindness. I am humbled to be able to work with such wonderful friends. I feel like I now have a purpose."

"Thank you, Mrs. Mogami." said Mayor Lugi. "This is a great day! Now all of you enjoy yourselves as we celebrate the winners!"

The marching band began playing and the fireworks were seen in the sky as the little village of Chevel acknowledged one of their own. Mrs. Mogami would be great for all these projects with her talent and teamwork.

"I'm so glad we decided to help Mrs. Mogami," said Kylie. "None of this would have happened if we had not invited her to lunch. "Yes," said Evelyn, "to think that it all happened because we went to visit Mrs. Mogami. Yes, a lot of positive things happened that day at the cottage at Deer Crossing."

Mrs. Mogami said Mayor Lugi. "I have one more question for you. We will need your first name so we can put it on your trophy."

Mrs. Mogami turned to the mayor and said….. "Glenda….My name is Glenda."

The end

Discussion Questions / fun facts

- Where did Mrs. Mogami's name come from? My daughter's 3 dogs. Monty, Georgia (abbreviated Ga) and Missi

- Where did Mrs. Mogami's first name (Glenda) come from (my sister)

- Who are the 6 friends? My 6 granddaughters: Kylie, Ellie, Rylee, Charlotte, Elaina and Evelyn.

- Who was the first animal that was to be adopted at the animal shelter? Chloe, our beloved Shih Tzu (14 years old)

- Where did the name Tuit lane come from? My 4 children live in Texas, Utah, Indiana and Tennessee

- Where did the name Kyelry come from? My 3 granddaughters are in Texas. Kylie, Ellie, Rylee (Kyelry county was named in my first book. (Fillmore the frog catches the fly. 2012 Authorhouse)

- Where did the name Chevel come from? My granddaughter Charlotte in Indiana, and 2 granddaughters (Evelyn and Elaina) in Tennessee. Charlotte, Evelyn, Elaina.

- Where did Mayor Lugi's name come from? My son's 2 dogs. Lucy and Gidget.

- Where did Everest the engineers name come from? My granddaughter's cat.

- Where did the name Mrs. Stiltner at the corner market come from? My mother's name.

- Who were the football players? My sons: Eric, Josh, Christopher and my son-in-law Nathan

- Who were the chefs at the cooking school: My daughters in law: Heidi, Abigail and Jill and my daughter Ashley

Printed in the United States
by Baker & Taylor Publisher Services